CORKERY SCHOOL
W9-BHR-830

Smooch Your Pooch

For my dear husband, Fred, and our own smoochable pooch, Barkly.

-T. S.

Library of Congress Cataloging-in-Publication Data is available.

ISBN 978-0-545-25551-6

10 9 8 7 6 5 4 3 2 1 10 11 12 13 14

Designed by Angela Jun
Printed in China 46
First edition, September 2010

Smooch *Your* Pooch

By Teddy Slater
Illustrations by Arthur Howard

Cartwheel Books®

SCHOLASTIC INC.

New York Toronto London Auckland Sydney Mexico City New Delhi Hong Kong

Smooch your pooch to show that you care.

Give him a hug
anytime, anywhere.

Toss him a bone.
Feed him some kibble.

Or better yet, pizza.
He'd sure like a nibble.

Get out your fiddle and play a sweet song.
Musical pups will love howling along.

HOWLELUJAH
CHORUS

Tickle his belly.
Rub his soft snout.

When he woofs at the door,
let him go right on out.

Some dogs love
to paddle.

Some dogs love to roll.

But all dogs love digging
a nice messy hole.

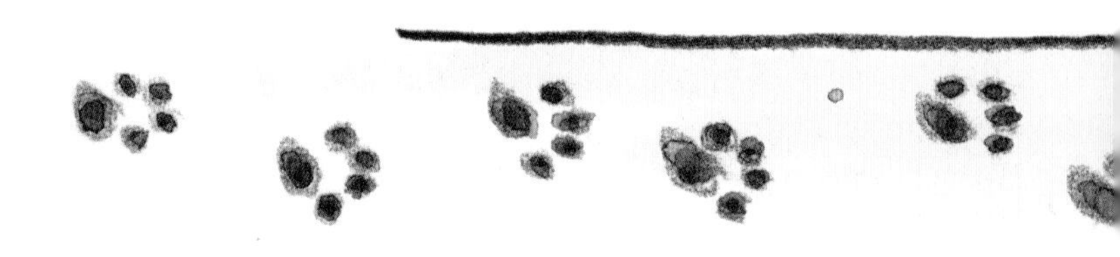

So, if he's your buddy,
just let him get muddy.

There are so many wonderful
things you can do
for the four-legged friend
who's so loyal to you.

Throw him some
tennis balls:

ONE

TWO

THREE

FOUR.

You can't throw too many –
he'll always want more.

Throw him a stick.
Throw him a Frisbee.

To make your dog happy,
you must keep him busy.

Take him along when you go for a hike.

Save him a seat
when you pedal your bike.

Let him sit by your side when you go for a ride.
And make sure that the window is opened up wide.

When his ears get all flappy,
you'll know your dog's happy!

When he's all tuckered out and it's time for a nap, give him some space on the couch

. . . or your lap.

Some dogs love
to snuggle.

Some dogs love to dance.

If yours wants to skateboard,
then give him a chance.

But most of all, love him
and give him a kiss.
He'll kiss you right back
with a smooch just like this.